Once Upon

The children wondered, "Where did the rock come from?"

Jeanette Kroese Thomson

AuthorHouse™
1663 Liberty Drive
Bloomington, IN 47403
www.authorhouse.com
Phone: 1-800-839-8640

© 2011 Jeanette Kroese Thomson. All Rights Reserved.

No part of this book may be reproduced, stored in a retrieval system,
or transmitted by any means without the written permission of the author.

First published by AuthorHouse 11/30/2011

ISBN: 978-1-4634-0847-3 (sc)

Library of Congress Control Number: 2011910958

Printed in the United States of America

Any people depicted in stock imagery provided by Thinkstock are models,
and such images are being used for illustrative purposes only.
Certain stock imagery © Thinkstock.

This book is printed on acid-free paper.

Because of the dynamic nature of the Internet, any web addresses or links contained in this book may have changed
since publication and may no longer be valid. The views expressed in this work are solely those of the author and do not
necessarily reflect the views of the publisher, and the publisher hereby disclaims any responsibility for them.

*Illustrations JTW , Jill Thomson Wright.

*The photos in the last part were taken by my husband, Gary A. Thomson and myself.

Dedicated to six grandchildren:
Calla, Griffin, Jess, Sionna, Maya and Amelia

Contents

Part One:
How The Earth Was Made   1

Part Two:
The Marsupians: Grandpa Wally's Tale of Origin   28

Part Three:
The Earth Was Sacred.
Human Beings Loved The Rocks   58

ONCE UPON A ROCK

*The children played upon the rock
and wondered, "Where did the rock come from?"*

The Hunnebedden Rocks in The Netherlands

14-10 Billion Years Ago
The Big Bang Break-up!
The Origins and Evolution of our Universe

5 Billion Years Ago
Our Planet, the SUN was forming.

4.6 Billion Years Ago

It is the **HADEAN EON** a Precambrian Super Eon.
The EARTH was born.
A planet as Red Hot as the Sun—8000 degrees F.
It was FIRE!
Meteorites from Space reigned down.
It was Radio Active. There are no rocks this old.

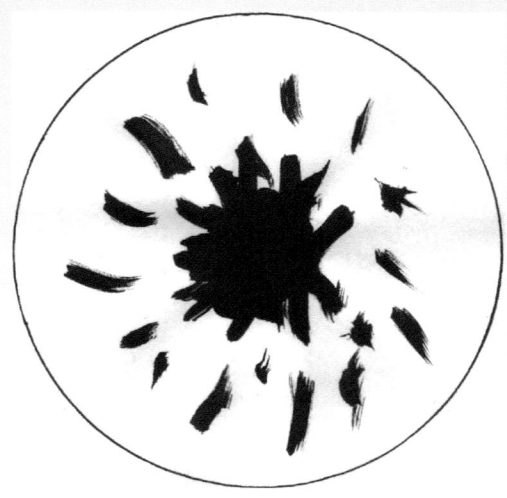

Then volcanos spewed the molten lava
from the center of the earth.

The Infant Earth writhed in volcanic eruptions
The very hot lava bubbled up to the surface of the earth.
The volcanoes began to cool.
VOLCANIC ROCKS were formed.
As they cooled they looked like pillows.

The heat from the rocks
radiated out and the rocks began to cool down.
As the volcanic rock cooled,
oxygen and carbon dioxide mingled together
to form WATER.
Then the carbon dioxide and water created clouds.

THUNDER
and
LIGHTENING
and
WIND
came.

4 Billion Years Ago

It rained for **millions** of years.
A vast, hot, dense OCEAN appeared
from all the water
that rained down.

3.5 Billion Years Ago

A new Rock,
GRANITE
began to change the surface of the Earth
that had been only Basalt Volcanic Rock.

Now a CONTINENT
began from the
Granite Rock.
There was Water and Rock
on the face of the earth.

The **EARTH'S SUN**
shone down all day
on the spinning EARTH!

The Moon began forming 4.5 Billion years ago

When the earth spun away from the sun,
the earth became very dark.
pulling it back and forth to create the TIDE.
The **EARTH'S MOON** brightened the dark sky.
The moon made friends with the water.

3.8 Billion Years Ago

It was the ARCHEAN EON Precambrian—simple life
3.5 Billion Years Ago—The Magnetic Field formed.

3 Billion Years Ago

THE OXYGEN REVOLUTION

In the shallow coastline of the Granite rock, where there was water,
the carbohydrates, from carbon dioxide and water
using light as energy, produced large amounts of OXYGEN.

2.5 Billion Years Ago

It was the PROTEROZOIC EON

Life adapted to oxygen and GREEN PLANTS began to form
from the rays of the sun, mixing with the rocks.
This is called PHOTOSYNTHESIS!
The plants used the carbon dioxide
and gave back OXYGEN.
And so, the Earth slowly began to change.
Blue water and **blue sky** appeared.

2.2 Billion Years Ago

The **Super Continent Rodinia** formed from the granite rock.
It was a desert and lifeless Rock.

1.5 Billion Years

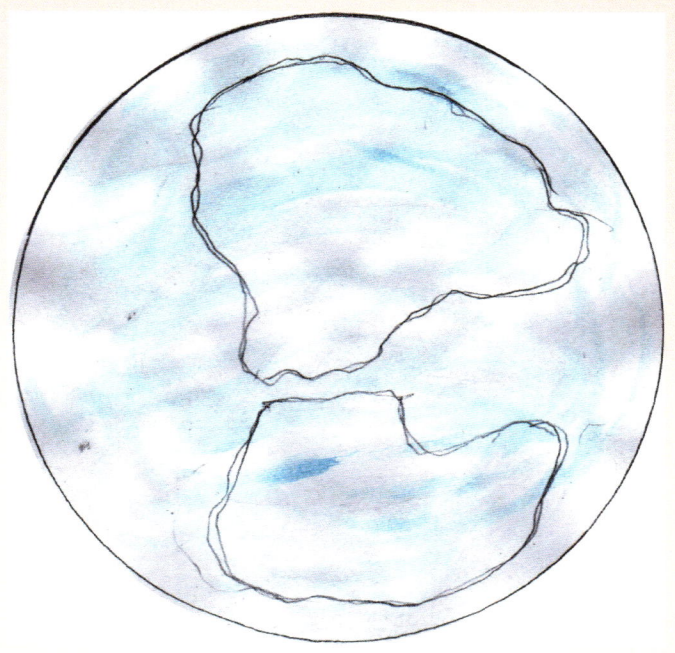

There was a Blue Ocean.
Rodinia began to break a part,
for the center of the earth
was molten hot liquid.
The crust of the earth broke a part.
There was the beginnings of two separate continents,
Laurasia and Gondwana.
The earth became very cold
and covered with ICE!
It was -40 Degrees F.
All marine organisms went Extinct!

600 Million Years Ago

Once again the molten lava began to force its way up
to the surface of the Earth.
The ICE began to melt and WATER appeared once more.

550 Million Years Ago
PHANEROZOIC EON

The **Vendian Period** brought complex soft bodied multicellular life.
It became a SEA OF LIFE!

544 Million Years Ago

It was the **PALEOZOIC ERA** and the **Cambrian Period**
with giant complex animals in the water.
The Burgess Shale in Alberta, Canada, tells the story.
There was the ancestral beginnings of North America
when Pannotia broke free from Laurasia.
Coral reefs appeared at the edge of the ocean.
Later, these ancient reefs would produce an energy called **OIL**.

510 Million Years Ago

The Ordovician Period and primitive fish appeared in the oceans.

441 Million Years Ago

The Silurian Period introduced the vertebra.
Life moved to the Land.
Big huge Plants began to grow!
All of the Land was in the Southern Hemisphere.
It was tropical and hot next to the Equator.
FRESH WATER on the land appeared from the huge plants.
It became a tropical SWAMP! As life expanded,
a layer of protection from too much light,
made the **Ozone layer**, protecting the Earth
from the Sun's harmful rays.

410 Million Years Ago

During the **Devonian Period** an ocean extended from Western North America and Alberta, Canada, to the Gulf of Mexico.
There were invaders from the sea and great tectonic movement
as Laurasia and Gondwana moved closer together.

353 Million Years Ago

Abundant plant life and huge trees grew on the lands
during the **Carboniferous Period**.
This would become COAL.
And much, much later, when HUMAN BEINGS
discovered the COAL and OIL
they would begin the INDUSTRIAL REVOLUTION.
The Earth provided the GIFT of ENERGY for the human being's needs.

.

300 Million Years Ago

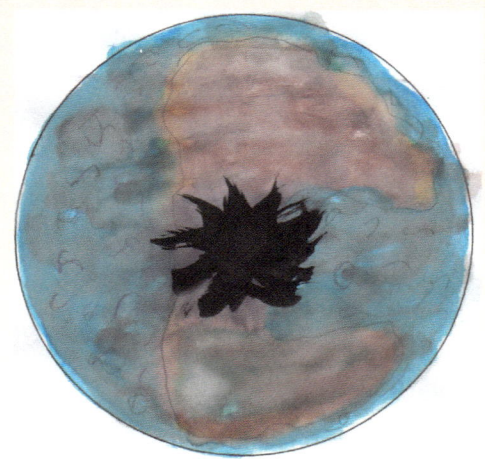

During the **Permian Period** molten lava
exploded through the crust of the earth.
90% of all earlier Cambrian LIFE went extinct!

250 Million Years Ago
The **MESOZOIC ERA** began with the **Triassic Period**.
Pangaea, the last Super Continent formed,
bringing Laurasia and Gondwana back together.

206 Million Years Ago
Life began once again!
The **Jurassic Period brought**
Tropical Forests and the Reptile Age!

Enormous insects, lizards. snakes, and alligators began.
The most giant of all, the warm blooded DINOSAURS appeared.
The rich environment of the Earth
that created huge tropical forests
allowed them to grow to enormous sizes.
They move from the sea to the interior land.

145 Million Years Ago

It is the **Cretaceous Period** and the Earth is active with volcanoes and earthquakes once again.
Many other rocks appeared
from the cooled lava called **IGNEOUS ROCKS**.

After being on the surface of the Earth, these rocks from the
weather of wind and rain and snow layered to become
SEDMENTARY ROCKS.

The Earth continued to quake,
so the rocks would be buried
down into the earth. They became
METAMORPHIC ROCKS.

MUD from weathering became a sedimentary rock called SHALE.
From the pressure and heat inside the Earth
the SHALE became SLATE, a metamorphic rock.
LIMESTONE, a sedimentary rock made from sand became
MARBLE, a metamorphic rock.

THE LARGE DINOSAURS BEGAN TO GO EXTINCT!

135 Million Years Ago

During the **Cretaceous Period** the Earth once again began to split apart.
Pangaea became **Laurasia** and **Gondwana** once again.

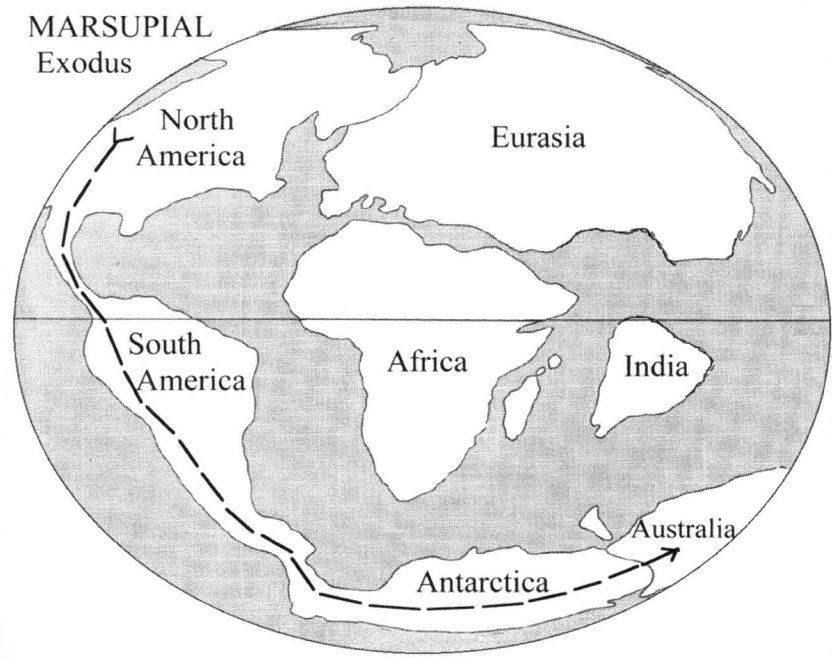

When Pangaea began to break apart
to Laurasia in the north and Gondwana in the south,
there was a land bridge for a **Marsupial Exodus**.
They moved through **South America** and **Antarctica** to **Australia.**
Some of the marsupials remained in South America.

70 Million Years Ago

The **CENOZOIC ERA** and the **Tertiary Period,**
ARC ISLAND from the PACIFIC OCEAN
moved East and pushed up against
the west side of the North American continent
causing the Rocky Mountain uplift.

65 Million Years Ago

During the **Paleogene Period** Continental formation of today stabilized.
When the large dinosaurs went extinct,
smaller remnants survived to fly and walk the earth.
The **Duckbill Dinosaur** roamed over a vast territorial range
from Alberta in the north and south as far as North Dakota.
The rise of **Mammals** began.

30 Million Years Ago

The **Neogene Period** began the environment of today.

25 – 12 Million Years Ago

During the **Miocene Epoch**, the Ape species
became present in **Africa, Europe and Asia**.

12 -3 Million Years Ago

The **Pliocene Epoch** began the origin of **Hominid** (upright) species.
The environment is open grasslands and savannahs.

10 Million Years Ago

There was the three-toed horse, the camel and the rhinoceros
found in volcanic ash next to an ancient waterhole on the
North American Great Plains.
Life evolved with the changing environment.
The animals that survived the break up
of the earth were dispersed to all the continents of the Earth.
Laurasia became **North America, Europe and Asia.**
Gondwana became **South America, Africa and Australia.**

3 Million Years Ago

The **Quaternery Period** began the Ice Age activity.
It was the **Pleistocene Epoch**.

JTW

3 Million to 10,000 Years Ago
The **Holocene Epoch** to the present age.

40,000 Years Ago
Modern **Homo Sapiens** emerged.

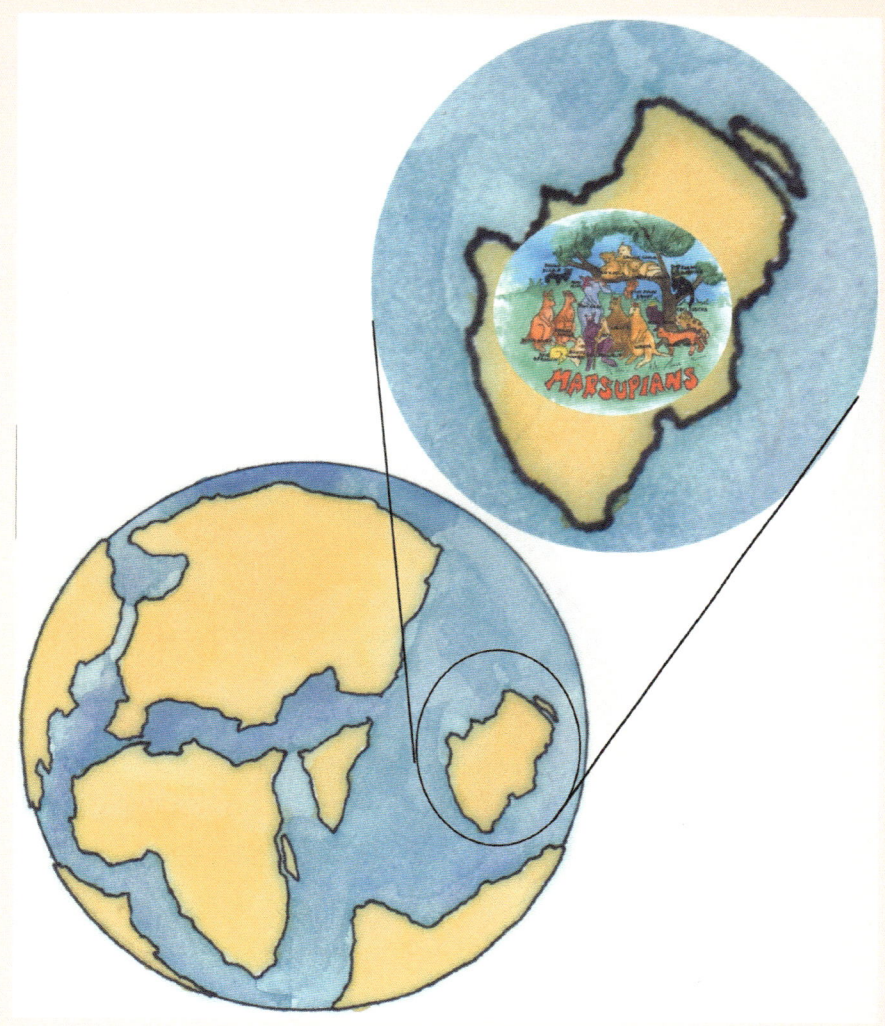

The Marsupial Family expanded and evolved
to the present day in Australia.

References

Burgess Shale fossils. (July 24, 2001) Department of Geology & Geophysics, The University of Calgary, Calgary, Alberta. http/www.geo.ucalgary.ca/ email: department @geo.ucalgary.ca.

Busbey III, A. B., R. R. Coenraads, D. Roots, & P. Willis (Rocks and Fossils). Brochu, C. A., K. Long, C. McHenry, J. D. Scanlon & P. Willis (Dinosaurs). *The Nature Companions Rocks, Fossils and Dinosaurs.* Consultant Editors: D. Roots. & P. Willis (Rocks and Fossils), M. K. Brette-Surman (Dinosaurs). San Francisco, CA: Fog City Press.

A beautifully illustrated and enjoyable study of Rocks, Fossils and Dinosaurs. A wonderful book for family and libraries.

Coppold, M. & W. Powell. (2000). *A Geoscience Guide to the Burgess Shale. Geology and Paleontology in Yoho National Park.* British Columbia, Canada: The Yoho Burgess Foundation.

Dawkins, R. (2004). *THE ANCESTOR'S TALE: A Pilgrimage To The Dawn of Evolution.* Boston, New York: Houghton Mifflin Company.

Dunning, F.W. and I.F. Mercer, M. P. Owen, R. H. Roberts and J.L.M. Lambert (1978). *Britain before Man.* Birmingham, England: James Upton LM.

Flood, J. (1983, reprinted 1988). *Archaeology of the Dreamtime: The Story of Prehistoric Australia and Her People.* Honolulu: University of Hawaii Press.

Gould, S. J. (1989). *Wonderful LIFE: The Burgess Shale And The Nature Of History.* New York: Penguin Books.

Gould, S. J. (2002). *The Structure Of Evolutionary Theory.* Cambridge, Massachusetts and London, England: The Belknap Press Of Harvard University.

A comprehensive study of the theory of evolution.

Smithsonian Natural History: The Ultimate Visual Guide To Everything On Earth. 2010. London, New York, Melbourne, Munich, and Delhi: DK Publishing.

Leinecker, R. (1994). *Developing Dinosaurs and Ancient Worlds*: *All You Need To Develop Your Own Dinosaur Park!* Indianapolis, IN: Sams Publishing.

Ludvigsen, R. Edited by, (1996). *Life in Stone. A Natural History of British Columbia's Fossils.* Vancouver: UBCPress.

Maher, Jr. H. D., G. F. Engelmann and R. D. Shuster. (2003). *Roadside Geology of Nebraska.* Missoula, MO: Mountain Press Publishing Company.

Manning, P. L. Foreward by T. Lyson. (2007). *Dinomummy*. Boston: Kingfisher.

Martin, L.D. & Illustrated by R. E. Bright. (1990). *Sea Monsters of The Midwest.* Lincoln, Nebraska: BrightChild Books.

McManus, J. R., Editor in Chief (1989). *Life Search: Voyage Through The Universe*. Editors of Time-Life Books. Alexandria, Virginia: Time-Life Books.

McPhee, J. (1998). *Annals Of The Former World.* New York: Farrar, Strauss and Giroux.

"The Cellars Of Time. Paleontology and Archaeology in Nebraska." *NEBRASKAland Magazine.* (January/February, 1994). Vol. 72. No. 1. Lincoln, Nebraska: Nebraska Game and Parks Commission.

Stein, S. (1986). *The Evolution Book.* New York: Workman Publishing.

A guidebook to observations, experiments, projects and investigations for children ages 10 – 14.

The Editors of Time-Life Books (1998). *Voyage Through The Universe—LIFE SEARCH*. U.S.A. & CA: Time-Life Books Inc.

The Smithsonian Chronicles has a DVD Series titled *How The Earth Was Made.* Previously aired on the History Channel, 2009. All Rights Reserved. 2010, Smithsonian Institute, Washington D.C., U.S.A.

Voorhies, Mike, Curator of Vertebrate Paleontology. "Ashfall: Life And Death At A Nebraska Waterhole Ten Million Years Ago." *Museum Notes,* Edited by Brett C. Ratcliffe. (February, 1992) No. 81, pp. 1-3. University of Nebraska State Museum.

Hundreds of skeletons of prehistoric animals have been found in a volcanic ash bed buried beneath the rolling farmlands of northeastern Nebraska. Some of the best-preserved fossil rhinos, horses, camels, and birds known anywhere have been, and are being excavated by Museum crews working in the Ashfall fossil beds in northern Antelope County.

Voorhies, M. *Ashfall Fossil Beds State Historical Park: Nebraska Wildlife Ten Million Years Ago.* Reprinted by permission of NEBRASKAland Magazine. University of Nebraska State Museum.

Windley, B. F. (1977, 1986). *The Evolving Continents.* Chichester, U. K.: John Wiley & Sons.

This book addresses the reader who has an understanding of basic geology and professional geologists who are interested in an interdisciplinary overview of recent advances in understanding of continental evolution.

Wood, D. (1996, January/February). "JOURNEY INTO THE EARTH. Cracking the Crust: Rock 'n' revelation." *Canadian Geographic, Vol. 116, No. 1, pp.48-59.*

The Lithoprobe investigation is Canada's largest national collaborative, multidisciplinary earth science research program. The University of Calgary is the site of the Lithoprobic Seismic Processing Facility which archives all the digital data since 1984 when the program began.
Lithoprobe scientists investigating geological puzzles in 10 Canadian areas. . . . . will gain a clearer understanding of the formation and four-billon year evolution of North America.

Once Upon A Rock

The *Marsupians*: Grandpa Wally's *Tales of Origin*

Once upon this particular pile of rocks in Australia, Grandpa Wally sat pondering. He pulled his walking stick up to his chin, making sure he placed the tip of his stick firmly in the familiar crevice of his favorite rock. These were not just any old rocks. These rocks went back, way back to the beginning of his family.

Grandpa Wally is a kangaroo—a Rock Wallaby Kangaroo. Kangaroos are marsupials. Kangaroo mothers carry their babies in pouches in the front of their bodies. In addition to kangaroos, other marsupials include opossums, bandicoots, and wombats. There is even a marsupial mouse.

Today most marsupials live on the continent of Australia.

But Grandpa Wally must tell and retell the Marsupians their Tale of Origin. And this will stimulate all the members of the clan to think about and tell their own tales of origin. Each one is unique from the other.

Wanda and Wally B., Joey's parents were still asleep over in a nice clump of grass. Little Joey's head suddenly poped up above the grass. Grandpa motioned him with a sh, sh, sh to follow him They were ready for an early morning walk-a-bout.

The morning sun is warm and bright. Grandpa Wally takes a long deep breath and closes his eyes for a minute just to feel the pleasure of being here one more time. This is his favorite spot in the whole wide world sitting on this big huge rock that lets him look-out over his big wide territory. He knows this place from his own childhood. Now here he is once again after the big long climb, enjoying it with his little grandson, Joey.

Grandpa Wally glances at Joey who has hopped a little way back from the edge of the rock. Grandpa can tell as he hesitates to come sit beside him that he is edgy "so to speak" about sitting too close to the precipice of this big rock that is very high over the valley below. This is Joey's first walk-about. Grandpa intends to introduce Joey to the history of the *Marsupian family*.

"I love this rock!" Declares Grandpa Wally with gusto.

"This is my favorite spot in the whole wide world. Come sit beside me Joey. Look how far we can see. You can even find where we came from this morning. If you look way over there, you might even see your mother, Wanda and your father, Wally B. down there eating their breakfast.

We got up so early this morning you can see the sun rising.

It was real dark when we left your mam and pap and now the sun's here. The shadows are almost gone.

Of course, this big rock always gives a shadow. In fact, when it is very hot, it is a place to find a cool spot to sit. This wonderful rock has been a protector for our family. I call it 'our sanctuary' because we always know this big red rock will be here. It never changes. This is where I tell our story. You know, I'm the storyteller of our clan."

Joey does not move. He just looks at Grandpa and pretends to give his attention to a hole in the rock. He sticks his foot down in the hole, then hops back up just a little distance from the hole.

Grandpa sits silently grasping on to his big old cane. He had to use the cane the entire trip up to the top.

"Joey is a good boy, he thinks. He has been patient with me going slowly up here to the top. Now I must go slowly with him as I share our family story. Maybe he is young yet to understand it. But on the other hand, if I wait too long, he may not want to hear it at all. I think I'll just start right in on my tale and see how it goes," Grandpa decides.

Grandpa starts tapping softly on the rock with his cane. He sees Joey's attention shift as his eyes move to the tip of his cane. Grandpa hops over a little closer to where Joey is sitting.

Suddenly he stops tapping with his cane, and begins a slow rhythm of humming.

"Um, Um, Um, Um, Now Joey, are you listening?" Grandpa bends down and looks into Joey's eyes.

Let me tell you 'bout a tale
t'was a long time ago

when the earth started movin
and a shaken to and fro.

well, we Marsupians were there
and we felt that pitch

of the ground separatin
and creatin a huge ditch.

Then the ocean appeared
dividing up the place,

South America and Africa
split apart with no trace.

Along with the big places
came the rest,

Australia, our home
secluded for a test,

of SURVIVAL, SURVIVAL.

Grandpa Wally's wailing of "survival, survival" made Joey sit up and pay attention to his face more closely. Grandpa intent on his story, seemed oblivious to Joey and moved on with his rhyme.

We found ourselves sailing
south with a spin.

And from that day of movin
there we've been with most our kin.

We are Mult-Marsupials
in shape and sizes too.

Great Greys, Reds and Wallabys
well, we are all kangaroos!

There are the wombats, and the cuscus,
and the dasyure cats.

There's Tasmi Wolf and Tasmi Devil
who know how to scat,

for **survival, survival!**
Percy Platypus, who is fish, fowl
and animal as well,
shows examples of all creatures
found around us for a spell.

You see, we don't mind our differences
we are happy in **di----ver----s---i----ty!**

For our uniqueness as Marsupians
has set us free !
We have learned to survive
and we have multiplied by three.

Grandpa pauses for a minute to get his breath. It seems his emotions have made him very tired. He sits up strong, to bring home his final message to Joey.

Looking directly into Joey's eyes, he begins the last part of his story.

But there's danger a foot
in recent days!

We are worried about survival
once again - **IT'S A CRAZE!**

SURVIVAL, SURVIVAL, SURVIVAL!

    Upon finishing his story, Grandpa Wally's big feet began to thump - thump - thump. Then his big old tail moved into the rhythm. His Big Deep Voice began humming---HMMMMM; HMMMMMMMMM: HMMMMMMMMMMMMMMMMM.

Joey sat quietly watching him with all the big thoughts from Grandpa's story swimming around in his head. Soon the warm sun and Grandpa Wally's humming put him into a deep sleep.

Grandpa continued to think about all the Marsupians as the sun shone down on them and moved higher into the sky. A flock of birds circled high above swooping down to get a closer look. Their swishing bird's wings, a gentle breeze moving through the cracks in the big rock and Grandpa's pounding Rhythm seemed to echo through the rock.

"The Marsupials would have never survived if they had remained all over the earth" he thought.

He knew it was because the earth began to separate millions of years ago, that a safe haven was created for his family. But now the safe haven no longer existed. The marsupials had to use their own strategy for survival even more than when they first found themselves isolated on the continent of Australia.

Until recently, the only placenta mammal beside the H.B.'s(Human Beings) that caused a problem was Dingo Diable, the wild dog. The European H.B.'s brought him along when they first arrived to help them herd their sheep and cattle. The sheep and cattle were never a problem because they were grass grazers.

Dingo, on the other hand, liked to pick a fight. Grandpa gave a shudder remembering how his tail was caught in the vicious mouth of a dingo many years ago.

Keep the message simple and clear," He mumbled under his breath."

So---------here Goesssssssssssssssssssss! But let's get back to the main Marsupian Message. "

All the heavy thinking made Grandpa extremely tired as well. His head went down on his paws and he fell into a deep dreamtime sleep. All the Marsupians began marching through his dream.

Meet Mini Mum Mouse, the oldest Marsupian.

The marsupials, The *Marsupians* first ancestor, Maxi Mate the mouse lived then. Grandpa Wally chuckled to himself thinking, "Little Mini Mum, brave little Mini Mum will insist on telling this story. Well, I guess it is her story and for another time and place. She may be the smallest of our clan, but she certainly is also the oldest."

Mini Mum is the mother of all the Marsupians because her mouse ancestors were roaming the earth when it was one of the big continents called Gondwana. The **H. B.s** found their bones way over in China today. When Gondwana split apart the bones of Mini Mum's ancestors moved East. And then Gondwana became South America and Australia. The other big continent, Laurasia became the home of all the dangerous placenta mammals.

But first, let me introduce one Marsupian who has survived in North America. Meet Opie, the Opposum. He's non-violent and has used a strategy for survival we can all consider.

When the going gets tough, you know what he does? He plays DEAD! It works every time. H.B.'s have been known to throw him in the trash can; kick him off their busy highways; let him be for dead.

But------when the dust settles and everything quiets down again, Opie gets up, shakes himself off, and walks away. Pretty good strategy, don't you think? From what I understand H.B. warriors, or soldiers (that's what there called now) have been know to use this strategy to stay alive as well!"

Grandpa gives off a rough cough, then settles back down to his dreamtime.

His thoughts move back to the rest of the clan.

Before I move along to all the Marsupial family in Australia, let me mention a few of our South American marsupial friends.

Grandpa Wally suddenly woke up because he was thumping his big ole tail!

He looked down and saw little Joey with his head resting on the big rock close by. He gently tickles his nose with his tail and Joey opened one eye. Then he gives out a big yawn.

Grandpa said softly to Joey, "Before we journey back down our big Rock, I have one more thing for you to put in your think-tank about your Marsupian family.

We have known how to survive for a very long, long time. Do you know why, Joey?"

Joey lazily looked up at his Grandpa. Grandpa too, found himself getting very tired once again. After all, soon he knows he must tell the Marsupian tale to the whole clan. But for now, a little rest would be very good. His head goes down onto his familiar rock into a deep sleep.

As Grandpa Wally moves back into dreamtime, he thinks again about the whole Marsupian Mob.

His oldest enemy/friend Tasmanian Wolf is no longer around, he sadly muses. Sometimes I miss him, even though we fought a lot. He had his good sides. For sure he cared about our family. In the end, he helped me fight off Dingo Diable. Somehow he knew I was in trouble. I'm really sorry he isn't with us now. H.B's say he's gone EXTINCT! That word is a BIG word with serious consequences. Grandpa Wally sighs in his sleep and gives out a silent snort of sadness.

Suddenly Grandpa Wally gives off a singing sigh. It's because his dream turns to the Coola Trio: Co Coola, Connie Coola and Cherry Coola. Three sweet and fun-loving Koalla, always laughing and singing. They bring such joy and happiness to the clan. They say,"'see no evil, say no evil and sing no evil" that's our motto.' We love the world. We love to live, especially in trees. When we are together, we are a team of three. That's our lucky number--THREE! Everything happens in THREE! Don't you see! One is Co; Two is Connie; and Three is Cherry: Let's say it again! ONE! TWO! THREE!"

Grandpa Wally chuckles in his dream because the Coola Trio is so consistent! Their song never changes. It may get boring at times, but one things sure, it's dependable. Co, Connie and Cherry are like three rays of sunshine--Australian Sunshine!

Grandpa Wally's dream moves on to other female members of the clan. All of them bringing a special flavor of sugar and spice. Of course some are more sugar and others are more spice.
Ceci Cuscus is a sugar type, Grandpa surmises in his dream. His image shifts to lovely Ceci with her creamy fur, perfectly tan spot. Her sweet little face is so pleasant to watch. And then there's her soft little purring voice. She never drives you crazy, but rather her voice kinda lulls one to sleep. Grandpa's sleep moves into a softer and warmer place dreaming about Ceci.

Grandpa Wally rolls over and suddenly his facial expression becomes more lively.

That's because his dream image changes to Sarah Dashure. Now, Sarah is another story. No messing around with her--that's for sure, Grandpa's experienced male judgment knows this. She may be very beautiful with her glissening black and white fur, but she's also a very tough lady. One word out of line from any male, will send her into a fury---a black and white fury! Grandpa's head shakes a little as he remembers times when Sarah got her steam up. She certainly is no mild and loving Ceci! Or sweet little things like the Coola Trio! With another final shake, Grandpa turns over to dream about his marsupian mates. Even though they can be hard to get along with--I know where they stand!

With that a line-up of all the single males came into Grandpa's dream: Doni Down Bandi, a marsupial bandicoot comes up first. He's rather schizophrenic.

He says, "If I could only climb a tree like Opie the Opposum, my distant relative in North America. Somehow my tail just isn't long enough anymore. I want to be up-side-down and look up at the sky. Instead I have these fears during the day that give me the big urge to go underground. Of course, I come out at night and eat all the wonderful greens on the ground. But I keep seeing all those leaves on the trees. Lots of my Marsupian Mates are up in the trees. Why can't I be there too! I have a positive phil-os-o—phy! Look Up! Look Up!" I say'

His favorite phrase rings forth: "**I would, if I could, and I CAN!**"

But, the other thing is, I have this fear. I'm not like Opie. He sits right out there and plays dead—even in the daytime! Not me, I have to be under the ground.

Tasmi Devil who left South America and bravely moved on to Australia is the vicious one! He just tackles anything that gets in his way. He takes on his enemy right up front. He can become so agressive that he even will chew off his own foot if it's caught in a trap to get away. Opie instead just lays there like he's dead. He is vulnerable to whatever happens. They are such opposites! The strange thing is that Opie probably comes through better than Tasmi Devil. I think he has the better way.

Grandpa Wally remembers that conversation with Doni Down. He contemplates the deadly virus that seems to be plaguing Tasmi these days here in Australia. He's a great fighter! I hope he can recover.

Grandpa's dream goes back to Doni Down Bandi. He has spread himself over a wide space between South America and Australia and he seems to be doing just fine, He decides with a happy grump.

Once again, Grandpa begins to chuckle. His dream has turned to Billy Wombat. Now here's a guy who will never give you any trouble. No big philosophical ramblings from him! He's a day-by-day sorta guy who just loves his life--especially on the beach--playing volleyball and surfing it up. His big yearning is the high waves, or the high life, so to speak! In fact, the higher the wave, the better. High waves means high surfing; high volley balls means harder spikes! "What is life all about?" says Billy. No wasting it with lots of talk--I'm into ACTION!

Grandpa's dream takes on a different view as he visions the two extremes of the two mates Opie the Opposum and Tasmi Devil--the one completely non-violent and the other very violent.

How can that be? Both from the same family of marsupials. Opie plays dead if he comes into a situation of danger.

Grandpa Wally's dreamtime finally moves to the last three members of the Marsupian clan.

They are the most reliable and stable ones: Big Tom Grey, the biggest and most experienced kangaroo who protects the clan. Beware to anyone wanting to cause mischief of Big Tom's flying punches and powerful kicks. He is a fantastic boxer, thinks Grandpa Wally. When he's around, there is no need to worry.

Then there's the magnificent twosome Rhoda and Rouge, the two red kangaroos. They have a confidence and goodwill that makes everyone feel at ease. So, with this positive note, Grandpa Wally's dreamtime slowly moved to a wakeup call from little Joey.

Grandpa all of a sudden jumped up on his hind paws, scooting Joey out of the way so that Joey had to sit up too.

"Listen to the last two lines of my story and put them into your loooooooong memory!

OUR DIFFERENCES MAKE US STRONG!
WE'VE KNOWN THAT ALL ALONG!

Did you hear what I said Joey? Repeat it with me!

OUR DIFFERENCES MAKE US STRONG!
WE'VE KNOWN THAT ALL ALONG!"

Chanting together "OUR DIFFERENCES MAKE US STRONG!
WE'VE KNOWN THAT ALL ALONG!" the young and old marsupial hopped together down the big rock.

References

Bergamini, D. et les Re'dacteurs des Collections TIME-LIFE (1964, 1969). Life Le Monde Vivant: Paysages Et Nature En Australie. Amsterdam, Holland: Composition par Draeger Freres, Paris Imprime en Hollande par Smeets Lithographers, Weert Relie par Proost and Brandt N.V.

Dawkins, R. (2004). *The Ancestor's Tale*. Boston: Houghton Mifflin Company.

Dawson, T. J. "Kangaroos." *Scientific American*. (August, 1977). Vol. 237, No. 1, pp. 78-89.
These hopping marsupial mammals have evolved in relative isolation for some 25 million years. Their adaptive strategies closely parallel those of the hoofed mammals of the semiarid Old World grasslands.

Great Book Of The Animal Kingdom with full-color illustrations of 750 species, their habits and environment. (1988). New York: Arch Cape Press.
A well illustrated and detailed encyclopedia of the animal kingdom with colored images and easy to understand text.

Larousse Encyclopedia Of Animal Life. (1980). Maurice Burton, Editor. Paris: Larousse & Company Incorporated.

McCord, A. ((1977). *The Children's Picture Prehistory: Prehistoric Mammals*. London: Usbourne Publishing Ltd.

Sharman, G. B. "They're A Marvelous Mob Those Kangaroos!" *National Geographic*. (February, 1979). Vol. 155, No. 2, pp. 192 – 209.

A wonderful and detailed article about the fascinating adaptive characteristics of the Kangaroo.

Skokstad, E. (2003, Dec. 15). "Mother of All Marsupials." *4 -- ScienceNow. WWW. http://sciencenow.sciencemag.org.*
Excerpts from this article:

Last year, the fossil beds of Liaoning Province, China, yielded the most primitive placental mammal ever found. Now comes another record-breaker: the most ancestral marsupial known, in such good shape that even some of the fur is preserved. (...) the mouse-sized fossil will provide a wealth of information on how the earliest marsupials evolved.

At 125 million years, the new fossil--dubbed Sinodelphys szalayi--pushes back the record of marsupials by 15 million years. (Molecular data suggest that the group could be as old as 190 million years.)

Once Upon A Rock
The Earth Was Sacred.
The Human Beings Loved The Rocks.

Earliest human ancestors used rocks as *tools*.

Human Beings Built Megaliths!

Carnac in Brittany

Orkney in Scotland

Duddo in England

Stone Age people who inhabited the Atlantic coast of Europe built megaliths! Mega-liths means big-rocks. These megaliths are really big. How did Stone Age people move such stones? How did they tip them up on end? How did they do it without modern machinery? There are thousands of big stones at Carnac in Brittany lining long avenues. What do these stones mean?

Giant Granite Menhirs of Brittany

Toppled & broken Grand Menhir of Brittany

Kerloas　　　Dol　　　Kerloas　Dol　Grand

The largest megaliths are called menhirs. These giant granite menhirs are found in Brittany on the west coast of France. The Grand Menhir stood 66 feet tall and weighed 350 tons (700,000 pounds). Today by comparison, the world's largest mining truck stands 47 feet tall, weighs 350 tons fully loaded, and is powered by a 3500 horsepower diesel engine. How did Stone Age people cut this huge stone from the quarry and then move it miles to its standing place? How many men and oxen were required to move such a massive granite pillar? And then, how did they raise this mammoth pillar into the sky 66 feet? Kerloas Menhir stands 33 feet tall on a high cliff; it was quarried and then pulled up the steep slope.

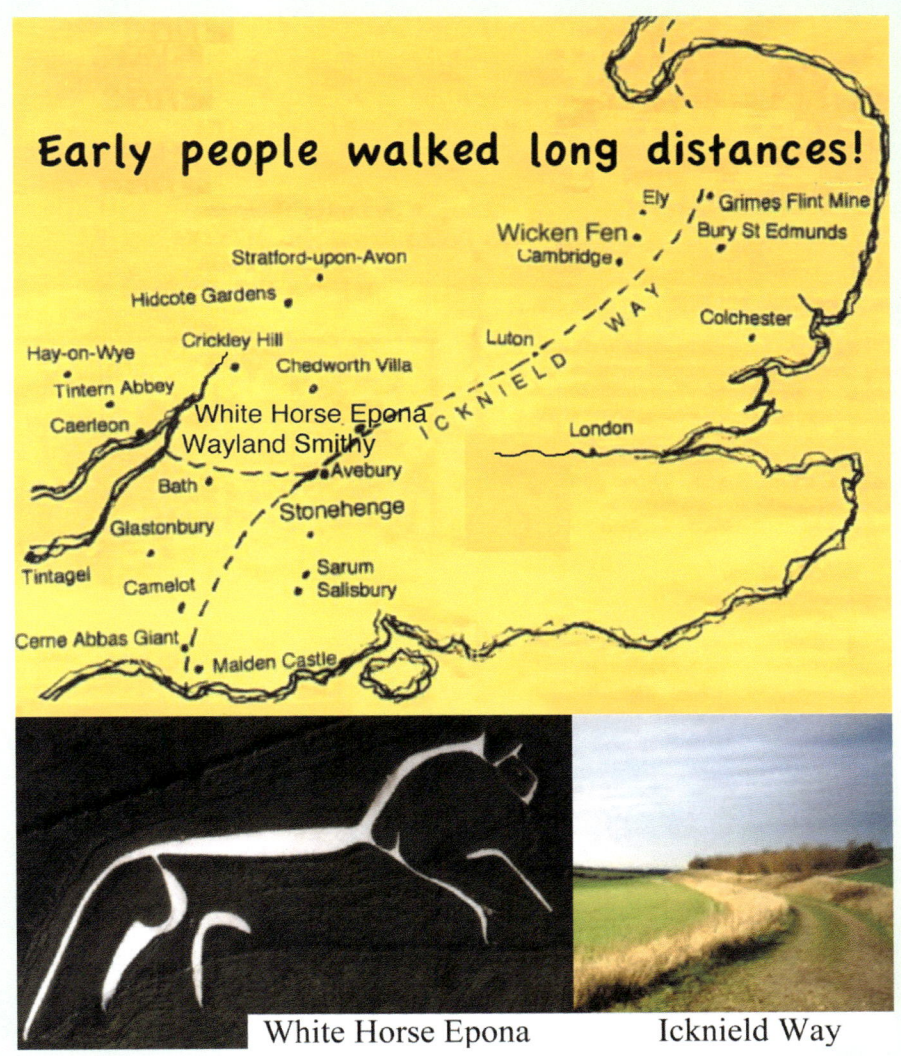

White Horse Epona   Icknield Way

Early people walked long distances. The Icknield Way crossed southern England. Carved in chalk and 375 feet long, the mythic White Horse Epona is high on the slopes of the ridge of the Icknield Way near Wayland Smithy's Barrow. Before sea level rose about 8000 years ago, one could walk from Ireland to the European Continent. The Icknield Way connected from East Anglia to The Netherlands before the North Sea encroached. Ecumenical language and myths networked Europe from the Baltic to the Mediterranean, from Ireland to India.

The Ancients Erected Dolmen Tombs!

Cornwall Quoit

Proleek Dolmen

Poulnabrone Dolmen

In the late Stone Age, people erected massive dolmen tombs to enshrine their dead. In Cornwall—the southwestern finger of England, dolmen were erected that are locally called "quoits." Geologically, the Burren in western Ireland is the uplifted ocean floor from a former world—the grey sedimentary rocks cover the region like a moonscape. How did the earliest Irish ever lift the 30-ton capstone onto the supporting orthostats of the Proleek Dolmen? How has the massive flat limestone of the Poulnabrone Dolmen survived the centuries, indeed, the millennia?

Humans Built Ceremonial Meeting Places

Humans built ceremonial meeting places in early times. The legend of La Roche-aux-Fées confirmed a marriage when bride and groom circled the rocks in opposite directions and counted out the same number of stones! Tristan and Iseult celebrated their love in Ireland, Cornwall and here in Brittany.

They Set Up Signposts For Havens

Early people traveled by boat. The king of Jorvik (York) was also the king of Orkney and king of Dun Laoghaire (Dublin)—overland impossible but viable by boat. To navigate they erected sentinel stones to guide the sailors to shoreline havens. The Neolithic Valley of Kilmartin on the western coast of Scotland was signposted but a tall sentinel stone visible to a approaching currach of visitors. Archaeologists today are finding fine crafted flints along the shorelines.

They made stone circles for fairs

Ring of Brodgar

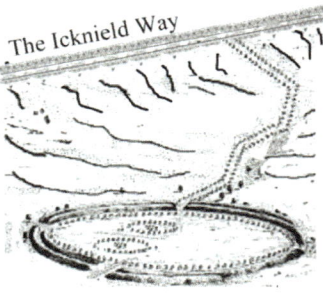

Avebury

Stonehenge

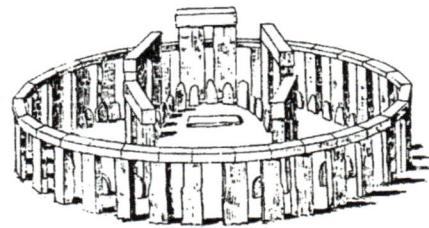

For their markets and fairs, early people constructed wide stone circles with avenues for parades. Avebury and Brodgar are excellent examples of well-designed massive stone circles. Circles within circles were an added feature as well as a deep moat around the perimeter. Avebury was adjacent to the Icknield Way—a cattle drover's ridgeway snaking its way across England. Of a more recent vintage, Stonehenge was built perhaps by a wealthy cattle baron.

They Chiseled Rock Art

Cornwall by the Sea

Ardmore by the Sea

Early artists chiseled rock art. In Cornwall on a high hill overlooking the Atlantic Ocean, an ancient artist sculpted a pillar and a bagel (donut). On the south coast of Ireland at Ardmore overlooking the Celtic Sea, a more recent Celtic sculptor discovered Eve and Adam within the granite rock. Before Patrick arrived in Ireland, earliest Celtic Christians were storytellers; these ecumenical bards easily intermingled Celtic and Biblical stories.

They Crowned Queens & Kings on Hilltops

Hill of Dunadd

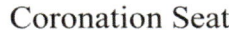
Coronation Seat

Ascent up to Dunadd

Celtic Boar on Seat

Hill of Tara

Lia Fàil Coronation Stone

They crowned queens and kings on hilltops. Dunadd was the oppidum of Scotland; Tara of Ireland. The royal palace on the hilltop was well-fortified with strong walls. At Dunadd the Scotti capital, the coronation seat had a Celtic boar inscribed. The coronation stone of Ireland, the Lia Fàil, had come with the People of The Goddess Danu from the Danube headwaters of Europe. The legend has it that a piece of the Lia Fàil was broken off to become the Scottish Stone of Scone at Dunkeld, a later Scottish capital. From there it was removed to Westminster Abbey where it is in the Coronation Chair

They Built with Stone Architecture

New Grange

Ur

Giza

Situated magnificently on a hill above the River Boyne, New Grange was the first designed and planned monumental architecture of Europe. In Egypt the monumental stone architecture of the Old Kingdom were the pyramids.

They built homes for extended families!

Skara Brae on Orkney

Scottish Broch   Double Walls

wind-hole 'window'
sleeping floors
fireside stories

They built homes—homes made of rock. For early peoples with a high mortality rate, homes were usually built for an extended multi-generational family. Skara Brae was covered by sand one evening in the Stone Age; a second storm in 1850 uncovered this settlement. The people had just been sitting down for supper and everything was there as it was 5000 years ago! Several apartments with lockable doors were connected by a community hallway. 2500 years ago the earliest Picts invented the broch—a double-walled round home with a fireplace on the first floor living area and a wind-hole at the top to let in light and let out smoke. Children could fall asleep on the upper floors while listening to fireside stories.

Early people wrote on rocks!

Aberlemno Stone

Ardmore Ogham

Algonkian Teaching Rocks

The Picts who invented the brochs also invented a codified picture writing. The Celts in Ireland wrote names and short phrases with ogham writing on rocks. In Canada the Algonquin Native People created the "teaching rocks."

The People Built Cathedrals & Castles

Chartres Cathedral

Le Baux

Provence

Human beings created magnificent cathedrals and splendorous castles. The white spires of Chartes Cathedral can be seen in the distance above the tree-lined road and waving wheat fields. Chartres has a soft feminine atmosphere. At Le Baux in Provence, the castle heights were dedicated to the Goddess.

Human beings continued to use rock to the present day. They made fences by choosing rocks that fit together without mortar. They called the method dry walls. The fences were strong and held the sheep inside. They would remove some of the rocks from the wall to free the sheep. There was no need for a gate.

Beautiful rocks have been found for jewelry: rubies, sapphires, opals, and the most precious diamonds. Metamorphic rocks have been quarried for sculpture like Michelangelo's' *David* and Constantin Brancusi's sculpture, *The Kiss*. From the rocks are valuable metals: iron, copper, and the most precious gold. Minerals have been found down through the ages with special value. At Hallstat high in the mountains of Austria the ancient Celtic people mined salt.

Today is the electronic age and we need rare minerals for our computers. The saga of *Once Upon A Rock* has no ending.

References:

Barclay, G. (1998). *Farmers, Temples and Tombs. Scotland in the Neolithic and Early Bronze Age.* Edinburgh, Scotland: Canongate Books.

Campbell, A. and D. Coulson. "Windows on the Past: Africa's endangered rock art provides glimpses of vanished worlds." *Archaeology*. A Publication of the Archaeological Institute of America. 2001, July, August, Vol. 54, No. 4, pp. 40-45.

Cook, D. & W. Kirk. (1995). *Pocket Guide Rocks & Minerals. 500 specimens, Fact Panels, colour-coding. The biggest little guide.* London: Larousse.

Dubois, R. (1968). *So Human an Animal*. U.S.A and Canada: Charles Scribner's Sons.

Gould, S. J. (1978). *Ever Since Darwin. Reflections in Natural History*. New York: W.W. Norton & Company.

Hingley, R. (1998). *Settlement and Sacrifice*. Edinbugh, Scotland: Canongate Books.

Leakey, M. (1984). *Disclosing The Past*. Garden City, New York: Doubleday & Company Inc.

Leakey, R. E. (1981). *The Making of Mankind*. New York: E. P. Dutton.

National Geographic BOOK OF PEOPLES OF THE WORLD. 2011. Washington D.C.: National Geographic Society.

Reid, R. (1977). *Picture Panoroma of World Building*. London: Mills & Boon Ltd.

Waechter, J. (1976). *Man Before History.* Oxford, England: Elsevier-Phaidon Publishing and New York: E.P. Dutton.

Author's Comments:

This book with it's three separate parts is discussing the total picture of *Once Upon A Rock*: the chronology of the earth; the biological migration of a particular and unique family of animals, the marsupials and how the crust of the earth--*rocks* have been used by human beings down through the ages to the present day.

The intention of the author is to allow space for the reader to contemplate and investigate our planet earth and the various ways of adaptation that has occurred by all living things. This process is ongoing and will continue. As human beings, we are blessed with a more complex brain that allows us to look at the total picture objectively. Freeing our thinking to do this sometimes requires a shift from an emotional and subjective exclusive view point to a more inclusive and more open approach. It is said that to engage in debate and exchange of ideas in a non-threatening sphere creates a process of growth and maturation. Our world has become an international community where many voices wish to be heard. The democratic and open society that we uphold in our culture will continue to adapt and change. This book intends to contribute to this attitude and good-will to look at "the other" as a friend.